Lilly Plays her Part

Brenda Bellingham

Lilly Plays her Part

Illustrations by Elizabeth Owen

FIRST NOVELS
The New Series

Formac Publishing Company Limited
Halifax, Nova Scotia

Formac Publishing Company Limited acknowledges the support
of the Cultural Affairs Section, of the Nova Scotia Department
of Tourism and Culture. We acknowledge the financial support
of the Government of Canada through the Book Publishing
Industry Development Program (BPIDP) for our publishing
activities. We acknowledge the support of the Canada Council
for the Arts for our publishing program.

Canadian Cataloguing in Publication Data

Bellingham, Brenda, 1931-

Lilly plays her part

(First novels. The new series)

ISBN 0-88780-500-0 (pbk)
ISBN 0-88780-501-9 (bound)

I. Owen, Elizabeth. II. Title. III> Series.

PS8553.E468L543   200   jC813'.54   C99-950278-6
pz27.B4142Li 2000

Formac Publishing   Distributed in the U.S. by
Company Limited   Orca Book Publishers
5502 Atlantic Street   P.O. Box 468 Custer, WA
Halifax, NS B3H 1G4   U.S.A. 98240-0468

Printed and bound in Canada.

Table of Contents

1
Too tall

We were crowded around the lockers getting ready to go out for recess. Our music period had just ended.

"I get to be Gretel!" I cried. "I can't believe it."

"You're the best singer in our room," Theresa said.

It was nice of her to say that. It's easier to be sorry for someone than glad. Theresa is my friend.

Our school was putting on a concert. The theme was "Fairy Stories." Our grade got to do "Hansel and Gretel." I

was going to be Gretel.
That's why I was so excited.

"Most people can't even sing in tune," Minna said.

Minna is my very best friend in the whole world. She is going to be a concert pianist when she grows up. That's why she knows about singing in tune. We didn't have to sing the whole play. Part of it was talking, but the singing was very important.

"I wish I'd got the witch's part," Theresa said. "I can do a great cackle. Want me to teach you, Minna?"

"No thanks," Minna said. She was going to play the part of the witch. Minna didn't sound very happy, but I was too excited to pay much attention.

Kendall was across the hallway at the boys' lockers, with his best friend, Heathrow. Kendall and Heathrow live on our street, so they're our friends, too, except they're boys.

"What are you so mad about?" Theresa asked Kendall.

"He's not mad," Heathrow said. "Let's go, Kendall."

Kendall shrugged Heathrow's arm away. "I AM mad," he said.

"Why?" I asked. Kendall had to play Hansel. He should have been as happy as I was.

"Why did Ms. Bell choose you to be Gretel?" Kendall

asked, scowling at me. "You're way too tall to be Gretel."

I HATE being tall.

2
Best friends

"Who says I'm too tall?" I asked.

People are always telling me how much I've grown. I wish they wouldn't.

"Lilly's NOT too tall," Minna said. "She only looks tall because the rest of us are so short."

Minna knows I don't like being tall, and I know she doesn't like being short. I'm her best friend, and she's mine.

"I'm Hansel in the play, and Gretel is supposed to be

my little sister," Kendall said.
"*Little* sister. Get it?"

"Shorty," Theresa teased
him

"Am not," Kendall shouted,
getting all red. "I'm average."

"Maybe Ms. Bell could
find someone else for Hansel,"
Theresa said. She eyed
Heathrow. "You're tall
enough."

Heathrow's cute and he's
very nice. Kendall clenched
his fists.

"I'm like you, Theresa,"
Heathrow said. "We can't
sing. That's why Ms. Bell
gave us the parts of the father
and stepmother. We only have
to talk. And Ms. Bell isn't
going to change *anybody*
with Kendall. He has a great

voice. He sings in his church choir."

"Wait," I said. "Kendall, do you have a pair of cowboy boots? They have higher heels. A lot of short men wear them. And I could bend my knees, or something. That way we'd kind of meet in the middle."

"Take out your pony tail, Lilly," Minna said. "It makes you look taller put up on top like that."

I ripped it out. "There," I said. "Is that better?"

"No," said Kendall.

"When I grow up, I'm going to be a doctor," Theresa said. "I bet I could chop a bit out of Lilly's legs and patch them into Kendall's."

"Gross," Kendall said.
Theresa loves gross.

3
Hansel and Gretel

Next day we had to practise
our play. Ms. Bell said we
should make up our own
words for the spoken part.
They'd be easier to remember.
The songs had to stay the
way she'd written them. In
the story, Hansel and Gretel's
father and stepmother are
very poor. Nobody has
enough to eat. They take the
children into the forest and
lose them. All the other kids
in our room were birds in the
forest.

"I wouldn't listen to my wife if she told me to lose my children in the forest," Heathrow said. "Fairy-story fathers are such wimps."

I *knew* Heathrow and I would see things the same way. "Right," I said. "Wimpy dads are from once-upon-a-time. These days, dads love their kids and help take care of them."

"There has to be a reason why Hansel and Gretel get lost in the forest," Ms. Bell said. "There has to be a reason for everything in a story. Things can't just happen."

"Okay," Heathrow said. "I'll go to another town to look for work. While I'm

away, their stepmother can lose them. She's wicked."

"Stepmothers in fairy stories always are," I said. "I don't know why. My stepfather isn't wicked. He's kind."

Ms. Bell blushed. "You know, Lilly, I've often wondered the same thing. I'm a stepmother myself. Maybe, as Hansel and Gretel are hungry, they could simply wander into the woods to look for berries and get lost."

"Hold it," Kendall said. "Hansel and Gretel wouldn't get lost. Hansel's a smart kid. He drops pebbles to show them the way home. Next time, it's breadcrumbs. It's not Hansel's fault those darned birds eat the crumbs."

4
Wicked step-mother

"Besides, it's not fair," Theresa said. "You can't change the story like that."

"We can change a few things," Ms. Bell said. "Before fairy stories were written down, they used to be told by storytellers. I'm sure each storyteller changed the details slightly. And fairy stories always get changed in movies."

"I don't care," Theresa said. "I *want* to be a wicked stepmother. Then I can scream at Hansel and Gretel when they spill the last of the milk. And I can take them into the forest and lose them. Everybody in a story can't be nice. It's boring."

In the end we took a class vote. Theresa and Kendall won.

When Kendall and I got to the forest, I sat on my heels and crawled around like a crab, so that nobody would notice I was taller than Kendall.

"Lilly, what are you doing?" Ms. Bell asked.

"Picking blueberries," I said. "They grow close to the ground. It's because we're hungry."

Meanwhile, Kendall hobbled around as if his

cowboy boots were burning him.

"Kendall, what's wrong with *you*?" Ms. Bell asked.

"These are my little brother's cowboy boots," Kendall said. "They hurt."

"I don't know why you have to wear cowboy boots," Ms. Bell said. "Hansel isn't a cowboy."

The birds started to giggle.

"Be quiet everybody," Ms. Bell said. "Lilly, stand up. I want you and Kendall to sing your duet. Kendall, hold Gretel's hand. She's your little sister and she's scared."

More giggles.

5
A sensible idea

Kendall's face got red as fire. "She isn't my *little* sister," he said. "She's too tall."

"Am not," I said. "You're too short. I'm bending my knees so much they're starting to wobble. You should get higher heels."

"I did," Kendall said. "I crumpled newpaper inside my heels to make them higher. My boots are killing me."

"Stop quarrelling," Ms. Bell said. "Birds, be quiet and get ready to sing your lullaby. Now, Lilly and

Kendall, hold hands and let me hear you sing."

Kendall barely touched my fingertips. I grabbed his hand, but he pulled it away. "Open your mouths," Ms. Bell said. "I can hardly hear you. And stand closer together. You're afraid, remember?"

I took one giant step sideways, and bumped Kendall. He almost fell down. Kendall glared. It was an accident, honestly.

Ms. Bell sighed. "Let's get on. Birds, Hansel and Gretel are going to sleep in the forest. The birds are sorry they ate the crumbs, so they cover the children with leaves to keep them warm. Then they sing a lullaby."

She had a bit of trouble settling the birds down. While she did that, Kendall and I 'discussed' our problem in whispers.

"Couldn't you get runners with platform soles, or walk on stilts, or something?" I asked.

"Why don't you shrink yourself in the clothes dryer?" he asked.

We were getting nowhere. "I have an idea," I said. "I can be your *big* sister and you can be my *little* brother."

"No way," Kendall said. "I'm older."

That's what I like about Kendall. He's so reasonable! I'm being sarcastic, in case you didn't know.

6
Heroines can have black hair

The kids who weren't birds wandered over to listen.

"So? Some younger kids are bigger than older ones," I said. "I knew two sisters like that. One took after her mom who was tall. The other was like her dad. He was short."

"I bet no one knew the tall one was younger," Kendall said.

He was making me mad. "Okay," I said. "What do *you* think we should do?"

"You could trade places with Minna," Kendall said.

"She's small. You'd make a great witch." He smiled at me.

Kendall should have been a crocodile. A crocodile always smiles — even when it's going to eat you. I'd like to make him into a crocodile purse, only it's not good to kill crocodiles.

"I couldn't be Gretel, anyway," Minna said. "Fairy-story heroines are blonde and blue-eyed."

"My mom's got a blonde wig," Theresa said. "You can borrow that, Minna."

Minna is oriental. She began to giggle. We all did. The idea of Minna in a blonde wig was too bizarre.

"Quiet, you people in the

corner," Ms. Bell said. "I can hardly hear the birds sing."

It's hard to stop giggling when you're told to stop. When we finally stopped for breath, I said, "Forget the blonde wig. Heroines can have black hair. What about Snow White? She had hair as black as ebony."

"Don't worry. I'd rather be the witch," Minna said. "I can hide behind my witch's costume. Heathrow lent it to me. It has a hat with a white wig, and a false nose with warts. No one will recognize me."

Minna is really shy, except when she's playing the piano.

7
For the sake of the team

Kendall and I had to pretend to find a cottage in the woods. It was made of gingerbread and candies, so we broke off a bit and ate it. That was when the witch appeared. Minna was the witch. She gave us food that made us go to sleep. While we were asleep, the witch put Hansel in a cage. She meant to fatten him up and eat him. Yuck!

Minna has a high, clear voice. She sings in the same church choir as Kendall. She was okay until she had to do her witch's cackle.

"She should have let me teach her how to cackle," Theresa whispered.

Minna is my best friend, but I have to admit that she made a super wimpy witch. Her cackle sounded more like a mouse squeaking.

"Try again," Ms. Bell said.

"Please, Ms. Bell, I can't cackle," Minna said. "And I can't scream. The sounds won't come out. Can't you find someone else for the witch?" She looked as if she was going to cry.

I nearly died of embarrassment for her.

"I'll do it," Theresa said.

"That wouldn't work," Ms. Bell said. "You're a good actor, Theresa, but we need someone who can sing."

"Lilly would make a great witch," Kendall said.

"Why didn't I think of that?" Ms. Bell beamed at me. "You have a strong voice, Lilly, *and* you can act. You're wasted on Gretel. She only sings duets with Hansel."

"But I don't want to be the witch," I said.

Ms. Bell put her hand on my shoulder. "Lilly, putting on a play is a team effort. It calls for self-sacrifice. The coach sometimes asks a hockey player to play another position — for the good of the team." She squeezed my

shoulder. "Go out there, Lilly, and be the witch — for the sake of the team."

Grrrrrrrr!

8
Witches do not have warts

I knew Minna's dress wouldn't fit me, so I found an old bedroom curtain with a ribbon threaded through the top for a skirt. It was gold. Mom lent me an old party blouse that she'd grown out of. It was gold, too, and really pretty. "Mom," I said. "Could I borrow your old blonde wig?"

"It's not that old," she said, "but you can borrow it if you like. Wait a minute. I thought you'd traded parts with Minna. A witch needs a white wig."

"Why?" I asked.

Mom shrugged. "I guess because she's old."

"Grandma's old," I said. "But she doesn't have white hair."

Mom chuckled. "Your grandma isn't a witch," she said. "And she colours her hair. But you can borrow the wig if you want to. See what Ms. Bell says about it."

The witch needed glasses, because she was short-sighted. She couldn't see that Hansel was giving her a chicken-bone to feel instead of his finger. Yeah! Right! I found an old pair of sunglasses lying around. Those would do.

The rehearsals were no problem. Ms. Bell said my witch songs sounded terrific. Theresa taught me to do a really wicked cackle. We didn't have to wear our costumes. The day before the concert we had dress rehearsal. I hid in a wash-room cubicle to change my clothes. I wanted to give everyone a surprise. I did that all right!

"A witch with blonde hair and shades!" yelled Theresa. "Are you crazy?"

"You look more like a fairy godmother than a witch," Kendall said.

"Where's your false nose?" Heathrow asked. "The one I lent Minna — with the warts."

"Witches do not have warts," I said. "Once upon a time, witches used to *cure* people's warts."

9
I look like a witch

"I saw a video of 'Hansel and Gretel,'" Theresa said. "The witch was played by a man. You could see his whiskers. He wore a false nose with humungous warts. Coo — ool!"

"Theresa, don't shout," Ms. Bell said. "Lilly, where is your white hair? I thought it was attached to your hat."

"It is," I said. "But I tucked it inside. It made me look like a witch."

"You're supposed to look like a witch," Kendall said.

"Not a Hallowe'en witch," I said. "Any witch who could change a bunch of kids into gingerbread children, could fix her own hair. She'd colour it, or rinse it with camomile, or something."

"Witches have white hair because they're old," Ms. Bell insisted.

"Not all of them," I said. "Even witches start off as babies."

"Babies can't be witches," Ms. Bell said. "It takes a lifetime to learn to be a witch. Believe me."

"Lilly," Minna said, "the witch in this story is evil. That's why Gretel pushes her into the fire. Evil is ugly."

"Yeah!" Kendall said. "The witch is the bad guy. Hansel and Gretel are the good guys. The good guys have to win. If you make the bad guy beautiful, the audience will get confused."

"What about Snow White's stepmother?" I asked. "She was beautiful. What about, 'Mirror, mirror, on the wall, Who is the fairest of us all?'"

"Lilly," Ms. Bell said. "Pull your cape around you to hide your dress. Take off that silly wig and shake down the white hair." Her voice was like steel. "Tomorrow is the performance," she said. "You'd better look like a real witch, Lilly. If you don't, I shall turn you into a toad."

10
The star of the show

We compromised. I didn't
wear the false nose with
warts. If you can't breathe,
you can't sing.

On the night of the concert,
Minna looked green. I hoped
she wouldn't throw up. I
hoped I wouldn't. I had to
hide inside the gingerbread
house and wait. When Hansel
and Gretel began to eat my
house, I crept around the
corner.

"Come inside, my dears,
and have something to eat," I
said to Hansel and Gretel.

"Don't go," yelled a little kid in the audience.

What was he trying to do? Spoil the story? Behind Hansel's and Gretel's backs, I shook my fist at the little kid. People chuckled. After that I didn't feel nervous at all. Playing the wicked witch was fun! I sang my first song and got a big round of applause.

When I made my wicked plan to fatten up Hansel to eat, I gave an evil cackle. When Gretel wouldn't work hard enough, I screamed at her. I saved my loudest, most ear-splitting scream for when Gretel pushed me into the oven. The audience gasped. They were really into it.

At the end of the evening, Ms. Bell came to our room.

"Congratulations, everybody!" she said. She beamed at me. "Lilly, you were an awesome witch."

"You were the star of the show!" Minna said, giving me a hug. She almost squeezed the breath out of me.

"You know, Minna," I said later. "I found something out tonight. Anybody can be a star. It doesn't matter if you're too tall, or too short, or what colour your hair, or eyes, or skin are. You don't even have to be pretty. It's not how you look that makes you a star. It's how you act."

We'll be doing a different play next year. I wonder what

part I'll get. I can't wait to find out. By the way, I decided not to make Kendall into a purse.

Meet four other great kids in the New First Novels Series:

Duff's Monkey Business
by Budge Wilson/ Illustrated by Kim LaFave
Duff is known for his vivid imagination. So when Duff announces he has discovered a monkey in the family barn nobody believes him. Just when everyone has had enough of Duff's tall tales a circus comes to town minus its star monkey. Could Duff be telling the truth after all?

Jan on the Trail
Monica Hughes/ Illustrated by Carlos Freire
When Jan and Sarah learn that Patch, their beloved dog friend, has been lost, they decide to become detectives and find him. Following the trail isn't easy but the girls are resourceful. They set off to follow the clues with the hope of reuniting Patch with his new owner.

Morgan's Secret
Ted Staunton/ Illustrated by Bill Slavin
When Morgan's best friend Charlie tells him a secret he swears he can keep one. But then Morgan is assigned Aldeen Hummel, the Godzilla of Grade 3, as his science partner and the trouble begins. Aldeen makes everyone nervous. She makes Morgan so nervous the secret slips out. What will Morgan have to do to stop Aldeen from blabbing? Will Charlie ever forgive him?

Robyn Looks For Bears
Hazel Hutchins/ Illustrated by Yvonne Cathcart
Robyn goes to her cousin's mountain tourist lodge near Bear Lake for the summer. She is determined to see a bear so she will have an exciting story to tell her city friends about her summer vacation. Robyn's quest for bears leads to lots of fun but no bears. Then when she least expects it her dreams come true.

Look for these New First Novels!

Meet Duff
Duff's Monkey Business
Duff the Giant Killer

Meet Jan
Jan on the Trail
Jan and Patch
Jan's Big Bang

Meet Lilly
Lilly's Good Deed
Lilly to the Rescue

Meet Robyn
Robyn Looks for Bears
Robyn's Want Ad
Shoot for the Moon, Robyn

Meet Morgan
Morgan's Secret
Morgan and the Money
Morgan Makes Magic

Meet Carrie
Carrie's Crowd
Go For It, Carrie